Written by Melissa Glim
Illustrated by Jennifer Glimcher

CreateSpace, Charleston, SC

With love and many moos!

The Littlest Cow

CreateSpace, Charleston, SC.

To Annie, my doggie muse.

In a village that's nestled 'tween mountains and fields,
The great cow parade is a very big deal!

Up and up Main Street, the heifers will stroll
and meet at the Common on top of the knoll.

"I want to march with the big cows, too!"
Said Annie, a little fox terrier who
Was furry and white, with brown and black spots.

"I'll fit right in! They'll let me! Why not?"

Big cows, tall cows, short cows, small cows,
Brown cows, black cows, cows with bright spots.

"Gee!" said Miss Annie, "I just love the whole lot!"

"Oh please, please, please! Let me march with the cows! I won't bark or bite. I'll moo! I know how."

So she went to the barn where the Holsteins live.
They were white cows with black spots,
  and boy were they big!

"Hey there!" said Annie. "I look just like you.
Do you think I could march in the cow parade, too?"

"Oh no," said the eldest cow with a snort.
"You're a dog and we never consort with your sort."

"In fact," said her friend, a young cow named Lynne,
"We don't even think Jersey cows should be in."

So Annie moved on to a field in the sun,
Where lunch for a herd of brown cows had begun.

"Can I join you and march in the big cow parade?"
Annie said to a kind-looking Jersey named Jade.

"No," shuddered Jade, "that parade's about us.
We don't want intruders there making a fuss."

"Those Holsteins are even too haughty and brash.
And I hear that some buffalo now want to crash."

Then Annie walked up to a hilltop all dappled
With twisted old trees that were hung with red apples.

She approached a tall hairy cow with a brogue,
Who had come here from Scotland to model for *Vogue*.

"Can I march with you?" Annie asked the Highlander.
"We'll have fun. I'll be good. I won't make a clamor."

"Nay," said the cow. "You cannae come along.
A dog in a cow parade simply is wrong."

Annie left feeling rejected and sad.
How could such nice-looking cows be SO bad?

"I still can't believe that these cows are all rotten.
Maybe it's just some bad hay that they've gotten."

"Or maybe the spring's rainy days got them down.
They all look so sweet when they're standing around."

"Or maybe," thought Annie, "they just have not met
Enough different cows and animals yet!"

So she took out an ad in
the town's *Daily Moos*,
Inviting all cows to a dance
at Old Lou's.

On Friday, the cows came to Farmer Lou's Barn
Where bales of fresh hay were set out on the lawn.

"Testing" - **SCREECH** - "testing!" Annie said in the mic.
"I'd like to welcome all cows here tonight."

She welcomed the other farm animals, too.
Like the sheep and the pigs and the owl who says "Hoo!"

Then a band took the stage, made of three alley cats
With a fiddle, a bell, and an overturned vat.

As the music began, the cows looked around,
And started to chat with their neighbors from town.

They talked about milking and where to find hay,
And which fields had shade on a hot, sunny day.

The Holsteins and Jerseys and Highlanders, too,
Found they had more in common than they ever knew.

As the night grew dark, the cows soon understood
That they're more same than different,
   and that it was good.

The cows and farm animals were happy to find
That their neighbors were all so friendly and kind.

"Miss Annie, you're great! You brought us together.
And now *all* the animals will be friends forever."

They debated and motioned and came to a vote:
Annie should lead the parade on a float.

The next day, quite early, the cows ambled down
To a field where they lined up to march through the town.

At the front of the line was an open Mercedes
Where Annie would ride wearing garlands of daisies.

Then a rumble of cheers rose up from the crowd:
"Hooray for Annie - our town's Littlest Cow!"

The End.

Mooooooo!

About the Author

Melissa Glim is a writer living in Maryland. She spent 12 years joyfully attending to her dog Annie's every whim. Every summer she returns to her hometown, Brattleboro, VT, where there really is a cow parade!

About the Illustrator

Jennifer Glimcher lives and works in Maryland with her family and cats Bella and Luca, but dreams of building a wild horse sanctuary out West. She began her artistic career in kindergarten.

And though they're not exactly sure how, Melissa and Jennifer are most definitely related.

29461655R00024